DK

A DORLING KINDERSLEY BOOK

Written by Angela Royston
Photography by Philip Dowell
Additional Photography by Dave King (pages 14-15 and 18-19)
and Jerry Young (pages 12-13 and 20-21)
Illustrations by Martine Blaney and Dave Hopkins

Aladdin Books
Macmillan Publishing Company
866 Third Avenue
New York, NY 10022

Eye Openers ™
First published in Great Britain in 1991
by Dorling Kindersley Limited,
9 Henrietta Street, London WC2E 8PS

Reproduced by Colourscan, Singapore
Printed and bound in Italy by L.E.G.O., Vicenza

1 2 3 4 5 6 7 8 9 10

ISBN 0-689-71519-6

Library of Congress CIP data is available.

·EYE·OPENERS·

Jungle
Animals

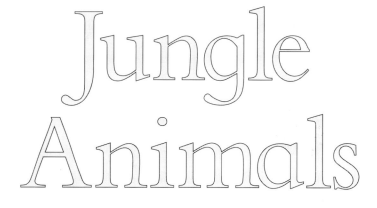

ALADDIN BOOKS
MACMILLAN PUBLISHING COMPANY
NEW YORK

Monkey

This monkey lives in
the jungle treetops. It uses its
hands, feet, and tail to climb
from branch to branch. Baby
monkeys ride on their
mothers' backs. Monkeys
eat fruit, insects,
and plants.

hand

face

tail

7

Jaguar

ear

A jaguar is a big cat that prowls through the jungle. It hunts smaller animals by hiding in the trees and pouncing on them from above. Jaguars also catch fish. They flick them out of the water with their paws.

8

fangs

tail

paw

9

Tree frog

leg

This tiny green tree frog is so small that it could sit on your thumb. It hides from its enemies among the green leaves. Tree frogs have sticky fingers and toes. They cling to leaves and twigs, looking out for insects to eat.

10

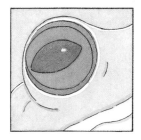

eye

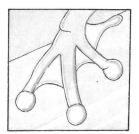

toes

 11

Crocodile

Crocodiles live near rivers or swamps and spend a lot of time in the water. Their powerful tails help them swim. Crocodiles use their jaws to snap up fish and other animals.

tail

scales

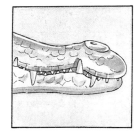

teeth

eye

13

Orangutan

An orangutan is a big ape with very long arms. It uses them to swing from branch to branch through the trees. Orangutans eat fruit and blossoms. Every night they make a nest from leaves and branches.

arm

hand

15

Toucan

Toucans are noisy birds that live in groups. They build nests in the treetops. Toucans use their giant beaks to pick berries and slice up soft, juicy fruits.

beak

eye

feather

17

Iguana

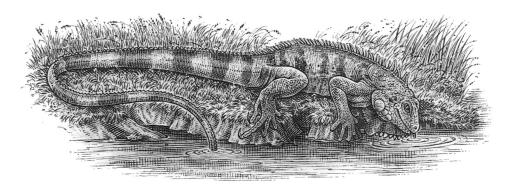

An iguana is a large lizard. It has thick, scaly skin. Iguanas eat leaves, flowers, and seeds. They are good swimmers and climbers. Every morning they climb high into the treetops to warm up in the sunshine.

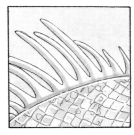

crest

tail

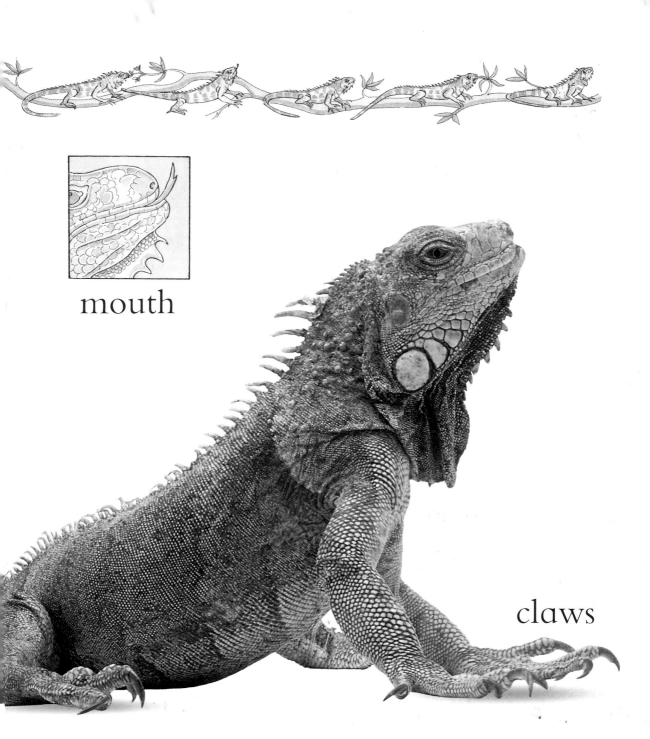

mouth

claws

Sloth

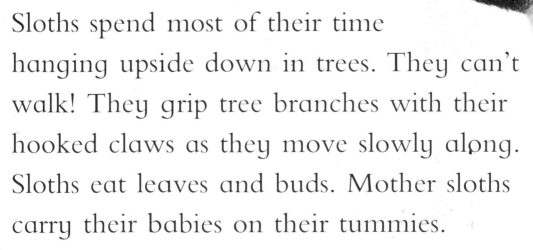

Sloths spend most of their time
hanging upside down in trees. They can't
walk! They grip tree branches with their
hooked claws as they move slowly along.
Sloths eat leaves and buds. Mother sloths
carry their babies on their tummies.

20

leg

arm

nose

claws

591.909 Royston, Angela
ROY
      Jungle animals

$6.95

DATE			